D1241164

This book belongs to

_____

Visit Little Lucy and Friends at www.littlelucyandfriends.com and www.playhousepublishing.com.

Library of Congress Cataloging-in-Publication Data
Jones, Katina Z.
Cool School Story / created by Deborah D'Andrea; author, Katina Z. Jones; clay illustrator, Jon Ottinger; dog photographer, Rick Zaidan.—1st ed.   p. cm.
Summary: Little Lucy and dog classmates use their imaginations to turn a story-building classroom activity
into an adventure with the help of Miss Bowser's magical word bones.
ISBN 1-57151-700-6
[1. Dogs—Fiction 2. Imaginatioin—Fiction 3. Storytelling—Fiction. 4. Magic—Fiction. 5. Schools—Fiction.]
I. D'Andrea, Deborah. II. Ottinger, Jon, ill. III. Zaidan, Rick, ill. IV. Title.
PZ7.J72045 Co2001
[E]—dc21   00-012848
First Edition 10 9 8 7 6 5 4 3 2 1
Printed in China.

Creator: Deborah D'Andrea, Ed.S.

Author: Katina Z. Jones

Clay Illustrator: Jon Ottinger

Dog Photographer: Rick Zaidan

Designer: Lynne Schwaner

Design Assistant: Kaycee Hoffman

PLAYHOUSE
PUBLISHING

Akron, Ohio

Little Lucy hopped onto her bike and began the trip to K-9 Elementary. She liked to play games of make-believe on her ride to school. One morning she would be a cowdog riding on the prairie. On another, she would be an astrodog flying to the moon.

On this particular morning, Lucy's thoughts were fixed on the game of Imagine-a-Story she and her classmates were to play that day.

When she spotted the school up ahead, Lucy pedaled extra fast. "Miss Bowser makes school so much fun," Lucy thought. "I hope she chooses me to be the lucky story dog!"

"Good morning, Class!" said Miss Bowser, as she picked up the Imagine-a-Story jar from the edge of her desk. She rattled the magical word bones that were inside and asked, "Are you ready to have some story fun this morning?"

Every dog howled, "Yip-yip-yippee!"

"Who wants to be the lucky story dog today?" asked Miss Bowser. Lucy raised her paw high into the air before anyone else in her class. "Hmm...let's see. How about Lucy?"

Imagine-a-Story
Day

Lucy scampered out of her chair so quickly that she skidded past Miss Bowser's desk and spun around in a circle. "Thank you soooo much, Miss Bowser!" said Lucy, as she gained her composure. Miss Bowser smiled with a gleam in her eye as she handed the Imagine-a-Story jar to Lucy.

Lucy pawed around in the jar looking for just the right word to get everyone started on their story adventure. "C'mon, Lucy!" yowled Petie. "We want a really cool story!"

Finally, Lucy took a deep breath. She reached inside the jar and chose one of the magical word bones. She slowly turned the bone over...

"Castle!" she shrieked. The rest of the class repeated the word, "Castle," and sighed as their minds filled with wonder and anticipation.

Lucy thought for a minute, then began her story.

"Once in a faraway land, there lived a king and a queen. They ruled over a kingdom where leashes were forbidden, dogs sat at the table to eat their scraps, and the ground was nice and soft—perfect for burying bones. Their castle was filled with toys and treats, and was surrounded by a beautiful river."

Dizzy couldn't contain herself and chimed right in. "There was a beautiful princess who always wore velvet-and-lace dresses and glimmering jewels," she said. "One bright summer day, the princess was playing in the garden, when all of a sudden..."

Petie continued the story: "...a prince from a nearby village rode in gallantly on his horse. Moonglow was the fastest horse in the kingdom. His coat was white and soft, and..."

"A-hem," said Dizzy, begging for attention. "Isn't the prince going to notice the princess?"

Shyly, Petie continued, "Of course, the prince couldn't help but notice the lovely princess playing in the garden."

"Oh, thank you, dear prince," said a regal-sounding Dizzy. She curtsied.

"After playing a game of "Go Fetch" together, the prince presented the princess with a diamond-studded dog collar and asked for her paw in marriage," said Lucy, winking at Dizzy. "To celebrate the engagement, the king threw a grand banquet," she continued, looking squarely at Verne, who perked up at the mention of food.

"Oh, yes! What a grand banquet it was," said Verne, licking his chops.

"The finest chefs in the kingdom were called upon to prepare bologna sandwiches, bologna milkshakes, roasted baloney bird, and, and...," Verne gasped for breath, "...and the largest serving of sausage-and-kibble casserole you have ever seen," he said, smiling broadly.

"Everyone had a wonderful time," announced Little Lucy. "Everyone, that is, except for Barkula, the evil wizard."

"You see, Barkula dreamed of one day marrying the princess himself. So seeing the princess with the prince made him very upset. He ran from the banquet, jumped onto his sorcery-spreading skateboard and began casting bad spells everywhere he went," said Spike, laughing mischievously.

"Oh really, Spike!" said Miss Bowser. The class barked its delight.

"He took away the princess' smile." Dizzy gasped.

"And he turned the prince's horse into a dragon." Petie frowned.

"And he even took away all of the bologna sandwiches from the castle." Verne moaned.

"But then, a fairy dogmother flew by. Miss Bowser, that's you,"
whispered Lucy. "She noticed that everyone was sad and crying at
the castle."

"The fairy dogmother immediately asked what was wrong," said
Miss Bowser.

"The queen told her about the princess' lost smile, the prince's horse
and—worst of all—the bologna sandwiches," said Lucy.

"The fairy dogmother assured the queen that everything would soon be alright," said Miss Bowser. "She waved her magic wand, breaking the bad spells, and sent the evil wizard to the doggie dungeon. Soon, everyone was happy again. The princess was smiling, the horse was no longer a dragon, all of the bologna sandwiches were back, and the castle was beautiful again."

"Yip, yip, yippee!" The dogs all cheered.

"The king and queen forgave the evil wizard and threw a huge party to celebrate," said Lucy.

"The fairy dogmother entertained the crowd with magic tricks. The now-reformed evil wizard and the queen led the others in the Walkin' Dog Shuffle.

Everyone ate bologna sandwiches and cheese and sausage and liver treats until their bellies were full and they all needed naps. The king..."

"Oh no, Verne!" shrieked Lucy, who looked back at "King Verne" just in time to see him lick his chops and dust off the last bit of crumbs from the "castle" word bone.

"I'm sorry, Lucy," said Verne sheepishly. "I just couldn't help it. All that talk about banquets and treats made me hungry." Everyone laughed, just as the bell rang for lunch.

"Oh, my delightful little friends, you have the biggest imaginations— no bones about it!" said a proud Miss Bowser. "What a deliciously fun story—right down to the last morsel!"

This book is dedicated to Joe, Noelle and David
my light and joy—DBD

Many thanks to the dog breeders and dogs
who helped make the book characters come to life:

Randy and Terry Stackhouse of Casa de Chihuahua, owners of Cordoba (Spike)
Mary Jo Baranowski of Primrose Poodles, owner of Mi Mi (Dizzy)
Mary Ann Holland, owner of Shakespeare (Petie)
Cathy Gillmore, owner of Lady (Miss Bowser)
and of course, my two dogs,
Lucy and Rico (Verne).

Special thanks to:

Jon Kapper and Jackie Wolf, editors extraordinaire,
who now know more about dogs than they ever thought possible.

Ann Longenecker, our talented costume seamstress.

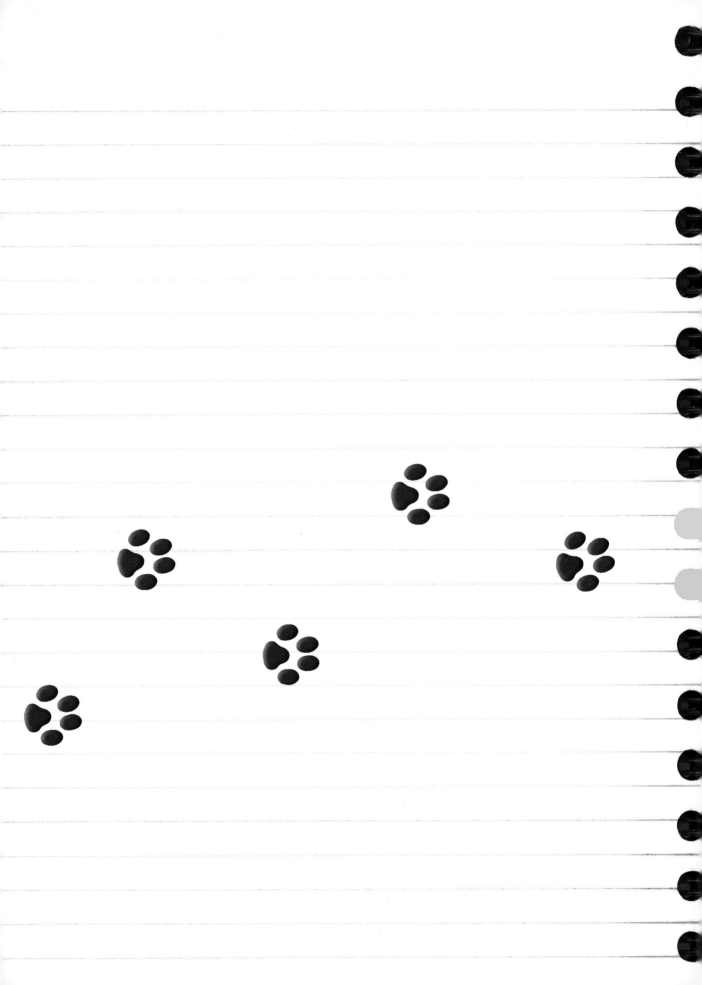